• I   N G •

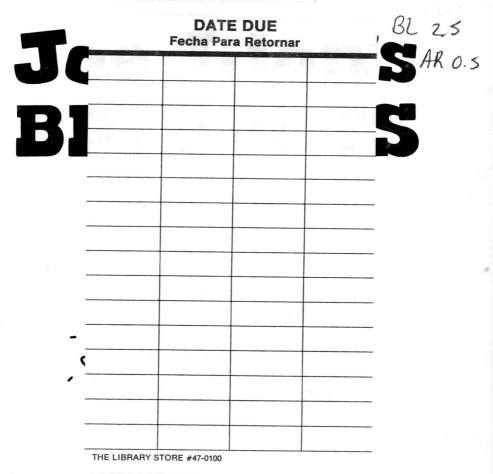

KARA MAY

Illustrated by
JONATHAN ALLEN

KING*f*ISHER

NEW YORK

W9-ASY-901

To Marian & Isobel
& Alasdair—J.A.

KINGFISHER
Larousse Kingfisher Chambers Inc.
95 Madison Avenue
New York, New York 10016

First published in 2000
2 4 6 8 10 9 7 5 3 1

1TR/0300/TWP/RNB/150ARM

LIBRARY OF CONGRESS CATALOGING-IN-PUBLICATION DATA
May, Kara.
Joe Lion's big boots / by Kara May ; illustrated by Jonathan Allen.—1st ed.
p. cm.—(I am reading)
Summary: Joe Lion, desperate to get bigger, acquires a
pair of boots that make him taller, but he soon finds that they
bring certain disadvantages and that he prefers being himself.
ISBN 0-7534-5318-5
[1. Size—Fiction. 2. Boots—Fiction. 3. Self-acceptance—Fiction.
4. Lions—Fiction.] I. Allen, Jonathan, ill. II. Title. III. Series
PZ7.M4524 Jo 2000
[E]—dc21
00-22567

Printed in Singapore

Contents

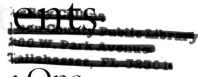

Chapter One

Joe Lion was small.

He was the smallest in his class.

He couldn't even reach the

goldfish to feed it.

"It's only me who

can't reach,"

said Joe.

He was the smallest in his family, too.

Big Brother Ben could reach
the cookie jar, easy peasy.

Sister Susan could reach it

easy peasy, too.

But Joe? He couldn't reach it,

not even on tiptoe.

"I'm fed up with being small,"
he said to Mom and Dad.
"I was small once," said Dad.
"You'll grow bigger one day,"
Mom told him.

But Joe wanted to be bigger NOW.

"I'll WISH myself bigger," he said.

He shut his eyes and wished.

He was still wishing when

he went to bed.

But the next morning, he was

the same small Joe Lion.

"Wishing hasn't made me bigger," he said.

"I'll have to think of something else."

He went to the big comfy chair

where he did his thinking.

What was this on the chair?

 It was Mom's new book,

How to Grow Sunflowers.

"Aha!" grinned Joe.

"That gives me an idea."

Big Brother Ben had a *How to* . . .

book—just the book Joe wanted.

He raced up to Ben's room.

On the bed he saw the book:

How to Build Yourself a Bigger Body.

Joe read through it in a flash.

To get bigger, he had to eat

a lot of food like pasta.

Mmm! Yum!

"I have to work out, too," said Joe.

"I know where I can do that!"

Chapter Two

Joe ran all the way to Gus Gorilla's gym.

Gus was big. Very big!

"Working out seems to do the trick,"

thought Joe.

"I can't wait to start," he said to Gus.

"What do I have to do?"

"You stand on this and run!" said Gus.

Joe ran on the treadmill.

Then it was onto the exercise bike.

After that, it was the rowing machine.

"Now, lift these weights, young Joe,"
said Gus. "Lift them good and high."

Joe's arms ached. His legs ached.

Even his little finger ached!

But he wanted to be bigger.

He picked up the weights.

He lifted them good and high . . .

until a weight fell . . .

CRASH!

"Yikes! It nearly hit my foot. That's the end of working out for me," said Joe.
But he was still determined to get bigger.

"Now I'm not working out," said Joe, "I'll do lots of extra eating to make up for it." Wherever Joe went, whatever Joe was doing, it was: MUNCH! CRUNCH! GOBBLE! At home:

MUNCH! CRUNCH! GOBBLE!

At school:

MUNCH! CRUNCH! GOBBLE!

On the bus:

MUNCH! CRUNCH! GOBBLE!

Even in the tub:

MUNCH! CRUNCH! GOBBLE!

17

"I have to be bigger by now," said Joe at last. He went to take a look in the mirror. He didn't like what he saw. "Oh, no," he groaned. After all that working out and eating, he was bigger, yes. Bigger-WIDER!

"But I want to be bigger-TALLER!"
said Joe.

Sister Susan had gotten bigger-taller
in just five minutes.

He asked her how she did it.

"I put on my high-heeled shoes,"
she said.

"Aha!" said Joe.

"That gives me an idea . . . !"

Chapter Three

Joe rushed into Ernie Elephant's shoe shop.
"I need some shoes to make me
bigger-taller," he said.
"Boots are best for that," said Ernie.
Joe tried on a lot of boots, but none
of them made him as bigger-taller
as he wanted.

"I can make you some," said Ernie.
"But it'll cost you, AND you have
to pay in advance."
Joe paid Ernie. "It's all the money
I have, but it will be worth it,"
said Joe.
"I'll bring them over—delivery
is free," said Ernie.

Joe couldn't wait
for the new boots
to arrive.
But at last, here was
Ernie. Now for the
BIG MOMENT.

Joe took the lid off the box.
He took out his new boots and
put them on.
"This is more like it!" said Joe.
He went to show the others.
"Surprise, surprise!
I'm a lot bigger-taller now."
They were surprised all right—
too surprised to speak!

Bigger-taller Joe could do a lot of things he couldn't do before.

He could reach the hall light. He turned it on and off—just because he could!

He could reach to swing from the rope.

He could see over Gus Gorilla's fence.

His new boots made a great noise, too!

CLOMP! CLOMP! CLOMP!

"I'll call them my Clomping Clompers," said Joe.

"That's a good name for them," said Mom.

But the next morning Mom said, "You can't wear those things to school!"

"I *have* to wear them," said Joe. In his Clomping Clompers, he wouldn't be the smallest in the class.

"I feel like an ant that's turned
into a giant," he said, as he headed
down the street.
Today was going to be his best
school day ever!

Chapter Four

Joe made his way to the bus stop.

"I like this bigger-taller me!"

he said.

He was closer to the

sky and could feel

the sun better.

He saw the bus coming,

and ran to catch it—or tried to!

In his Clomping Clompers, he could

only: CLOMP! CLOMP! CLOMP!

The bus went without him.

Joe was late for school.

Mrs. Croc wasn't pleased.

"I'm sorry, Mrs. Croc," said Joe.

"It was my Clomping Clompers."

"May I feed the goldfish?" he asked.

But the goldfish was already fed.

At recess, his friends were playing
soccer. Joe was good at scoring goals.

But not in his Clomping Clompers.

Joe was glad to get home.

"Cookie jar, here I come!"

He reached it, easy peasy.

Now it was time to watch his favorite

TV show, *Super Lion in Space*.

But then Mom said, "Hang up your

coat, Joe. You can reach the hook

in your Clomping Clompers."

And that was just the start of it.

Joe could reach a lot of things
he couldn't reach when he was
small Joe Lion.
Like the kitchen sink:
"It's your turn to do the dishes,"
said Big Brother Ben.

Like the toy shelf:

"You can put your toys up there

yourself," said Sister Susan.

Doing the dishes! Cleaning up!

"It's all I seem to do these days!"

said Joe.

But he couldn't do much else

in his Clomping Clompers.

Later, Joe's friends were off to the park.

"Are you coming, Joe?" they asked.

Joe shook his head.

He couldn't join in the games.

"I can only clomp!" he said.

"I'm going for a walk."

Joe clomped off down the street.

CLOMP! CLOMP! CLOMP!

But what was up with Jeff Giraffe?

"He looks like he's in trouble!"

said Joe.

Chapter Five

Joe soon discovered that Jeff

WAS in trouble.

"Goofy giraffe that I am,

I've locked myself out," he said.

"I came outside to pick some flowers,

and I left the bathwater running!"

Joe saw the problem at once.

Left to itself, the tub would overflow

and Jeff's house would be flooded!

Joe spotted the bathroom window—

it was open!

"You can get in up there," he said.

Jeff pushed his head through the window.

"But my bottom half won't fit,"

said Jeff. "The window's too small."

"Leave it to me," said Joe.

He knew what he must do.

First, off with his Clomping

Clompers.

Now, it was
Super Joe Lion
to the rescue!
Up the downspout.
In through the
window.

The water was rising fast—

and a lot of soapy bubbles with it!

"I have to do something!" Joe reached

for the stopper.

It was too far down.

He would have to go in!

He got up on the side of the tub
and jumped.

SPLASH!

He couldn't see through the bubbles
and he was running out of breath.
But he had to get to the stopper.
"Got it!" He pulled the stopper and
out it came.
The water gurgled down.
GLUG! GLUG! GLUG!
Joe whooshed the bubbles
out the window.

Then he slid back down
the downspout.
He saw a crowd had gathered.
Mom and Dad were there, and
Brother Ben and Sister Susan
and Gus and Ernie and
Mrs. Croc and all his friends.
They were waiting for news.

Quickly, Joe told them:

"Jeff's house is safe from flooding

with bathwater and it's safe from

bubbles, too!"

They all gave a cheer.

"Hurrah for Super Joe Lion!"

Joe felt very proud.

He was Super Joe Lion—just
as he was. He didn't need his
Clomping Clompers.

"My clomping days are over," said Joe.
"Being me is best. I don't want to be
bigger . . . well, not yet!"

About the Author and Illustrator

Kara May was born in Australia where, as a child, she acted on the radio. She says, "Even though I am grown-up now, I am still the smallest in my family, so I know just how Joe Lion feels." Kara used to work in the theater and has written a lot of plays for children, but now she writes books full-time.

Jonathan Allen played bass guitar in a band before he graduated from art school. He says, "When I was young I wanted to be a famous rock star, like the one in the poster on Brother Ben's bedroom wall." Now Jonathan is well known for illustrating children's books . . . but he does still play his bass guitar!

If you've enjoyed reading *Joe Lion's Big Boots*,
try these other **I Am Reading** books:

ALLIGATOR TAILS AND CROCODILE CAKES
Nicola Moon and Andy Ellis

BARN PARTY
*Claire O'Brien and
Tim Archbold*

THE GIANT POSTMAN
Sally Grindley and Wendy Smith

JJ RABBIT AND THE MONSTER
Nicola Moon and Ant Parker

KIT'S CASTLE
Chris Powling and Anthony Lewis

MR. COOL
Jacqueline Wilson and Stephen Lewis

MRS. HIPPO'S PIZZA PARLOR
Vivian French and Clive Scruton